PUFFIN BOOKS

Jeremy Strong once worked in a bakery, putting the jam into three thousand doughnuts every night. Now he puts the jam in stories instead, which he finds much more exciting. At the age of three, he fell out of a first-floor bedroom window and landed on his head. His mother says that this damaged him for the rest of his life and refuses to take any responsibility. He loves writing stories because he says it is 'the only time you alone have complete control and can make anything happen'. His ambition is to make you laugh (or at least snuffle). Jeremy Strong lives in Somerset with a flying cow and a cat.

LAUGH YOUR SOCKS OFF WITH

Jeremy STRONG

BEWARE! KILLER TOMATOES

Illustrated by

Rowan Clifford

PUFFIN

PUFFIN BOOKS

Published by the Penguin Group
Penguin Books Ltd, 80 Strand, London WC2R 0RL, England
Penguin Group (USA) Inc., 375 Hudson Street, New York, New York 10014, USA
Penguin Group (Canada), 90 Eglinton Avenue East, Suite 700, Toronto, Ontario, Canada M4P 2Y3
(a division of Pearson Penguin Canada Inc.)
Penguin Ireland, 25 St Stephen's Green, Dublin 2, Ireland (a division of Penguin Books Ltd)
Penguin Group (Australia), 250 Camberwell Road, Camberwell, Victoria 3124, Australia
(a division of Pearson Australia Group Pty Ltd)
Penguin Books India Pvt Ltd, 11 Community Centre, Panchsheel Park, New Delhi – 110 017, India
Penguin Group (NZ), 67 Apollo Drive, Mairangi Bay, Auckland 1310, New Zealand
(a division of Pearson New Zealand Ltd)
Penguin Books (South Africa) (Pty) Ltd, 24 Sturdee Avenue, Rosebank, Johannesburg 2196, South Africa

Penguin Books Ltd, Registered Offices: 80 Strand, London WC2R 0RL, England

penguin.com

Published 2007
17

Text copyright © Jeremy Strong, 2007
Illustrations copyright © Rowan Clifford, 2007
All rights reserved

The moral right of the author and illustrator has been asserted

Set in MT Baskerville
Made and printed in England by Clays Ltd, St Ives plc

British Library Cataloguing in Publication Data
A CIP catalogue record for this book is available from the British Library

ISBN: 978-0-141-32058-8

This is for Maria Baker, her family and all the staff and patients of the Children's Hospital, Bristol Royal Infirmary.

I would also like to thank everyone at the Big Ted Appeal and staff and patients of the Children's Department at RUH, Bath. It is a privilege to be involved with you all.

Contents

1. How I Ended Up in Hospital   1

2. How to Make a Mangospoon   11

3. How to Talk with an Alien   23

4. How to Demolish a Pyramid   33

5. How to Make a Promise, Maisie-style   46

6. How Not to Score a Goal   57

7. How to Escape from Hospital   67

8. How to Make an Entrance   74

9. How I Start Investigating   86

10. How Not to Conduct an Investigation   95

11. How Princess La-La Saved My Life   109

12. How to Win a Holiday   119

1 How I Ended Up in Hospital

Is life wonderful? No. Am I enjoying myself?
No. Am I surrounded by disease and despair?
Yes. Which is hardly surprising, because I'm in
hospital. Again. Do you think I like coming here?
No. In fact I take great pains to try and avoid it
but somehow, somehow, I always seem to end up
here, often with a great pain.

Mum says I'm a walking disaster. Dad says I
don't have accidents. 'You're an accident waiting
to happen, Jack,' he told me. 'In fact, you *are* an
accident.'

'A Jackcident,' sniggered my little bro, Ben.
The whole family laughed. Even me.

You'd think I was tied to this hospital with
elastic. The moment I escape – boyoyoing! I
come zooming back. Dad says he's plain fed up.

'I'm fed up with you ending up in hospital,'
he says. (See, told you.) 'I spend more time here
than I do at home, all because of you.'

'Dad, you're exaggerating.'

'Not a lot. You were here a few weeks ago with a broken foot.'

'It wasn't broken, Dad. It was badly bruised.'

'And last term you had an operation.'

'The doctors didn't operate, Dad. They thought they might have to, but they didn't.'

'I don't know why you swallowed that coin in the first place,' Dad said.

'Ben said it would stop my hiccups if I put a cold coin on my tongue.'

'That is unbelievably stupid.'

'I know that now, Dad, but I didn't know when I did it. I only realized how stupid it was when I swallowed it by mistake. Anyhow, it was Ben who said it. He's more stupid than me.'

'No, you're more stupid than Ben. He only said it, and he's seven, but you actually went and did it, Jack! And then it went straight down the toilet! Talk about chucking money away.'

Parents are lovely, aren't they? There you are on your death bed and all they can think about is money. I could have been choking my way to heaven!

ME: Uhuhh! Urhurrhh! URRRHHH! Dad! (*CHOKE CHOKE CHOKE*)

DAD: Just tell me where the money is, son! TELL ME WHERE THE MONEY IS! Oh, now you're dead! What did you go and die for? Wake up!

Yep – that's all the sympathy I get. I'm always having accidents. Some people reckon I am just humongously clumsy. Others think I'm plain stupid. But I can tell you this for sure – I don't do it on purpose.

So I'm stuck in hospital, again, and you would not believe how boring it is. What's the most boring thing you can think of? Socks? School? Auntie Rachel? Whatever it is that you are thinking of I can tell you now it's not boring enough because my boredom is as BIG AS A PLANET. (Jupiter probably – the biggest planet in the universe.)

HELP! I AM DYING OF BOREDOM! I NEED VISITORS! (But not Ben – he just winds me up.) Just to prove how bored I am, I miss school. Exactly. That much. I even miss

my teacher, Mrs Fetlock, and that's saying something. Do you know what her favourite subject is? Repetition. Here are a few examples of things she constantly repeats.

'Did you hear what I said?' Secret silent answer: *What?*

'Are you listening to me?' Secret silent answer: *No.*

'Jack Lemming, what did I just say?' Secret silent answer: *Jack Lemming, what did I just say?*

So I am lying here, on my back, twenty-four hours a day. Not allowed to move. Broken leg. Bad break. Top half of the leg, where the big bone goes, the femur. I may never walk again. My life lies in ruins, and my leg lies in plaster. Takes about six weeks to heal – four of them on my back, 24/7, leg covered in bandages and a giant bag of sugar hanging off my foot.

That's how doctors cure a broken leg. It's true. They hang bags of sugar from your toes.

Yeah – gotcha!! Had you fooled, didn't I? OK, here's the truth, and I mean the true truth. There is a weight hanging from my foot, but it's not a giant bag of sugar. It's a bag of . . . well, actually I don't know what's in the bag. Could be jam. Or dynamite. Or someone's brain, left over from an operation. Yuk. What's in the bag isn't important, but the weight is, because it helps to keep the leg stretched and straight. It's called traction.

Most broken legs aren't mended like this any more, not in plaster and everything. The doc pins it – not pins like you have at home – big steel pins. You don't feel it because you get anaesthetized first. When you wake up it's all been done.

Unfortunately, and that should be my middle name, *unfortunate* – Jack Unfortunate Lemming – my leg couldn't be mended the new, easy way of course. The break was complicated, and the leg got shoved into plaster. Typical. Will I ever get a lucky break? Ha ha. Lucky break! A hospital-type joke. There might be more of those. Don't say you weren't warned.

So I lie here festering and rotting away. Now I know what it's like to be an apple left in the fruit bowl for weeks and weeks, slowly going mouldy.

And what have I got to look at while I'm lying here? I will tell you – a small TV and the ceiling. If I turn my head to the left I can see the rest of

the ward I'm on. It's not all that big. Opposite
me there's Kirsty, although I call her Princess La-
La. She thinks she's above everyone else because
she's thirteen and goes to secondary school. Big
deal. Kirsty has multiple food allergies and all
she gets to eat is some horrible slop-stuff. It looks
vile but she says she doesn't care because at least
it stays inside her.

I said, 'How do you get multiple food
allergies?'

'I was born with them, if you must know,' she
muttered. Honestly, having a conversation with

Kirsty is like jumping into a patch of stinging nettles, so I shut up after that. Liam didn't though. Liam never shuts up. He said, what if you're not allergic to the food? Suppose it's the food that's allergic to you? She said he was stupid.

'Is that a medical definition?' he asked.

'In your case, yes,' said Kirsty (aka Princess La-La). I think she won that argument. Rats. She usually wins. Double rats. Still, it can't be very nice for her. There are loads of things she's not allowed to eat. Chips, ice cream, chocolate, cheese – that's just a few. Sometimes she has really bad weeks and can hardly eat anything without being ill. Then she has to come into hospital and get fed on the slop-stuff.

There are two other beds: one's empty and the other is *inhabited* by Liam (already introduced). I say inhabited because Liam lives in his bed a bit like a caveman in his cave. His bed is a mountain of sheets and covers and pillows and books and toys and I don't know what. Liam sits in the middle of it all, staring out, picking his nose and making 'ugg-ugg' noises. I'm not quite sure what's wrong with him, apart from being a complete clown. I did try asking. I said, word for word: 'Why are you in hospital, Liam?'

He said, word for word: 'Can't find the way out.'

See? I told you he was a clown. He reckons he should be going home soon. 'Can't be soon enough,' said almost anyone who heard him. He's a laugh, Liam, and I need all the laughter I can get because this place is killing me, and I don't think hospitals are supposed to do that, are they? They're supposed to make you

better, to help you live – but I am DYING OF
BOREDOM. I've said that already, haven't I?
That's how bored I am. I hope I get out soon.
I've got to get out.

I suppose you're wondering how I broke my
leg in the first place, and that's where things
start getting edgy. Everyone thinks I came off
my mountain bike and it's true, I did. The thing
is though that nobody knows *why* I came off
my mountain bike. That's why I have to get out
of here, get out before they come to *get me*, and
they will come, I know they will, because they
know what I did. I'm not brave enough to tell
you everything yet, but I will, I promise. All I can
say at the moment is that it was a tomato-related
accident. And someone died. And it was my fault.

2 How to Make a Mangospoon

Liam and Princess La-La have only been here
a week so far. Loads of people have come and
gone since I've been here. There was Charlie
who had his ears pinned, Beatrice who had one
leg stretched to make it as long as the other,
Tony who had unidentified spots, Jenny who had
her tonsils out, Grace who wouldn't say what

was wrong with her (but we all knew and I'm not telling) and lots more besides. You just get to know them and then they've gone home, all except for me.

Now then, if I turn my head to the right I can see . . . and this is quite exciting . . . I can see . . . the wall! Way-hey! Yeah! Cool! A whole wall. My excitement cannot be contained.

But wait, it gets even better because, if I look up (which is by far the most comfortable position for me, since I am lying on my back), I can see the ceiling! Great, the ceiling. It's like the wall really, isn't it, only it's above instead of at the side and there's a lot more of it, a great expanse of flat, cream desert. It's not exactly what I would call interesting. How many times do you rush home thinking, *I can't wait to get back and look at the ceiling!*

One of the things we did in History at school was learn about the sort of homes posh people lived in two or three hundred years ago, and one of the things they did was paint pictures all over their ceilings. They didn't paint them themselves of course because they were posh. They got other people, some not-at-all-posh people, to

do the painting for them. Mrs Fetlock took our
class on a trip to Bling House – 'So you can
see how civilized people lived,' she explained.
'People who knew how to handle a knife and fork
properly,' she added, eyeing Megan Morgan very
coldly.

'I want to be a knife thrower in a circus
when I grow up,' Megan explained. 'I was only
practising.'

'I don't remember them throwing forks as
well,' snapped Mrs Fetlock. 'Besides – it's very
dangerous.'

'That's the whole point, Mrs Fetlock. It wouldn't be exciting if it wasn't dangerous, and I wasn't doing it with a real person. It was only a dinner lady's apron.'

Mrs Fetlock ignored her. 'Bling House is famous for its painted ceiling,' she explained. 'I've always wanted to see it myself. I'm really quite excited and I'm sure you are too.' She beamed down the coach at us. We didn't beam back.

We wandered all round Bling House, which had an awful lot of stairs, and finally we came to this great big hall and the guide said that if we looked up we would see the most beautiful painted ceiling in the country. 'People come from all over the world just to see it,' she said.

We looked up and there was this massive picture above our heads. Well! No wonder people came from miles around to stare at it. There were all these ladies with nothing on! Dancing about all over the place. What a way to behave! There were cherubs too – you know, baby angels – and they weren't wearing anything either, not even nappies. And a chariot pulled by two horses, charging across the ceiling. You could see

all their underneath bits. It was a bit much. Mrs
Fetlock went very red and started talking rapidly
about the floor.

'It's made of very special wood. Look at
the pattern in the wood, Class Six. Isn't it
fascinating? I have never seen such a fascinating
floor. Quite amazing.'

'Did civilized people always go about with nothing on, Mrs Fetlock?' asked Megan, still staring at the ceiling along with the rest of us.

'Fascinating . . .' muttered Mrs Fetlock, crouching even lower to study the totally un-fascinating floor.

'I expect the posh people were so posh they could have the central heating turned up all year and they didn't need to wear clothes,' suggested Harvey.

'The one by the waterfall looks like Mrs Douglas when she takes assembly,' Megan pointed out, much to everyone's amusement. Mrs Douglas is our headteacher, and Megan was right. The lady by the waterfall had her arms stretched out on either side, which is what Mrs Douglas does in assembly when she's telling us to love our neighbours. (She should try living near Mr Tugg. He lives down our street and he's a maniac!)

'Is that the time?' cried Mrs Fetlock. 'Come on, Class Six. We'll miss lunch if we don't hurry. Follow me, this way.'

That was our school trip, and what I reckon is that we ought to paint our ceilings to make them more interesting. I wouldn't want ladies like the ones at Bling House, or even horses or whatever. It would be a bit much to be staring up at something like that. Suppose you had a herd of cows thundering overhead? You might get whopped by a passing udder. You'd have to wear a hard hat.

So, nothing like that – but you could have cars! Whopping great monster cars with flames belching from their exhausts, tyres squealing and scattering stones. Or jungle animals – leaping tigers, crashing buffalo, slithery snakes, mad monkeys and rainbow parrots chattering through a forest of rain-dappled leaves.

And even if people didn't do things like that in their own homes you'd think they'd do it IN A HOSPITAL WHERE MOST OF THE PATIENTS HAVE TO LIE THERE STARING AT THE CEILING ALL THE TIME!!!

It would be really good to paint the ceiling above my bed, and I did have a go myself a week or so back. I was SO cheesed off and I told Liam about Bling House and we worked out a plan to redecorate the ward, starting with the ceiling. We had several problems to overcome.

Problem 1. We didn't have any paintbrushes.

Problem 2. We didn't have any paint.

Problem 3. We didn't have any ladders to
climb up to reach the ceiling, and anyhow I
couldn't move from my bed so I would need
paintbrushes tied to very long poles.

Problem 4. Nobody would let us do it anyway.

So we gave up on that idea pretty quickly. But
then the next day Miss Crispin comes round
– she's the hospital teacher – and I was looking
at the book she gave me about the Romans and
there was a picture of a mangonel. (I think that's
how you spell it.) You might be surprised to learn
that you know what a mangonel is. You may
not know that a mangonel is called a mangonel
(I certainly didn't – until I saw that book), but
you do know what it is. It's that giant spoony-
catapulty-thingy that the Romans used to fling
great big boulders at the enemy.

There you are, you DO know what it is! I can
hear you at this very moment going: Yeah, of
course, the giant spoony-catapulty-thingy!

So I saw this picture in the book about the

Romans, and I thought, that's it, that is how we paint the ceiling. We use a mangonel – a miniature one, using hospital spoons. And for paint, we will use . . . hospital food. Am I brilliant? Yes!

I told Liam and he said: 'That's just what I was thinking.'

'Of course you were,' I grunted.

The next day we tried it out, when the staff weren't looking. Acne-Man had brought us some horrible stodge for lunch. (Acne-Man is one of the male nurses. His real name is Ashley, but I call him Acne-Man. You'd think the hospital wouldn't allow someone with a face so full of pimples to work with the walking wounded, but they do.)

Anyhow, I filled my spoon with mashed potato mixed with green peas. I put the spoon on my tray with the handle poking out over the

edge. It made a perfect miniature mangospoon.
I brought down my hand pretty sharpish
– whump!

PEEYOWW! SPLATT! That peasy potato
went whizzing through the air! Brilliant! You
should have seen it.

Unfortunately it went nowhere near the
ceiling. It hit the opposite wall, just above
Princess La-La. It looked as if someone had
suffered a spectacular sneeze. Then Liam took a
turn and his dollop of macaroni cheese created
a fantastic galaxy effect on the ceiling. It looked

good, but sadly it didn't stay up there for long. A few minutes later the biggest lump came unstuck just as Acne-Man passed underneath. Acne-Man keeps his head shaved so he got the full effect of a macaroni galaxy landing on his bonce from a considerable height.

Hilarious! Acne-Man felt his head, looked at the splattered macaroni on his hand and almost jumped out of his skin because he thought the macaroni was bits of his brain. (Might have been an improvement!) Then he saw the splodge on the ceiling. There was a long pause as he tried to figure it out. He swung round and stared accusingly at Liam.

'What?' went Liam, but it was obvious he was involved because he couldn't stop laughing.

So that was an end to our brave attempt to redecorate the ward. At least it helped pass the time. As you can see, we have to make our own amusements in here. After that everything went back to normal – or to put it another way, boring. Tedious and – scary. Trouble is, there's nothing to do in here except think and when I think my head immediately fills with tomatoes and a pair of feet. I am in deep, deep trouble and I've got to get out of here.

I should be allowed up pretty soon. I get
physiotherapy for a while to get the leg working
properly and after that I should be able to go
home. I hope so. Every day when the doc comes
and does his rounds I wait for him to tell me I
can get up, but he hasn't, not yet, but it must be
soon, it must be, it's got to be. Got to. Because if
it isn't soon I am going to be in big trouble and
I mean BIG trouble, with THEM, the police.
They must know it was me that did it – that
business with the tomatoes and the body. He
wasn't moving, not a flicker. He couldn't. Not
beneath all those tomatoes, because they weren't
just ordinary tomatoes. They were tinned.

3 How to Talk with an Alien

Hospitals can be strange places, especially at night. Odd things happen in the dark hours. Last night I was visited by a creature from another world.

Her name is Maisie, which is an unusual name for an alien. She didn't tell me herself. In fact she didn't say anything the whole time she was here, but she is definitely from another world. I don't mean a world in our own solar system and I don't mean our galaxy. Not even our universe. She is from a completely different universe. In fact, quite probably, where she comes from isn't even called a universe. It's probably called a *Qwrrrkknnikk*, and her planet is probably called *Spplinng*. Or something. Who knows?

At any rate she is definitely an alien, and she was under my bed. I've no idea how she got there. Maybe she teleported herself. It was evening and Acne-Man had been in and pulled the curtains. Princess La-La and Liam slid further down into their beds, lucky whatsits. If only I could do that, but of course I'M NOT ALLOWED TO MOVE! Just in case you'd forgotten. Sorry to keep going on about it, but you try lying on your back for four weeks – bet you can't even manage five minutes. I don't like to complain and I'm not complaining – I'm stating a fact, a fact of my life.

I lay in bed in the semi-dark, watching cows that weren't really there fly across the ceiling. Then, out of the corner of my eye, I saw a head appear beside me, low down, right at bed level. It was an orange head. It kind of levitated upwards and just appeared there, hovering at my side, staring at me. So I yelled. As you do when you've had a nasty shock.

'AAARGH!'

That woke everyone, including Princess La-La. (Good.) The lights went on and Acne-Man came pounding across.

'What's up?'

'It was Jack,' whined Princess La-La. 'He screamed.'

'Are you all right, Jack? Was it your leg?'

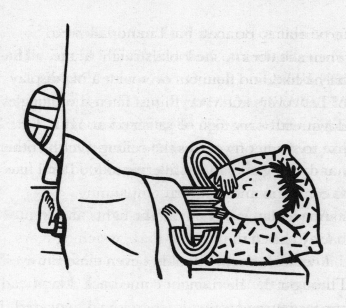

'No. I thought I saw . . .' I paused. I don't
know why, but I didn't want to say I'd just seen
an orange space creature hovering at the side of
my bed. So I told them I'd had a dream. Maybe
I had.

'Don't have it again,' sniffed Princess La-La.
'You woke me up.'

'I don't know what dreams I'm going to have,'
I said.

'You are such a pain,' she groaned, turning
on her side again. She does that on purpose
– turning on her side. She knows I'd love, love

to be able to do that, but I'm not allowed. So when she does it, she looks straight at me, all ha-ha-ha-like, and flounces over with a big display of bedcovers and everything. Then she snuggles down with a big sigh of satisfaction. Huh! I'd like to see her fly across the ceiling. On the other hand, I'm glad I'm not allergic to food and have to eat the slop she's given.

Acne-Man switched off the lights and went back to his desk.

I couldn't sleep. I couldn't even close my eyes. I thought the alien might come back. I kept my face turned towards where she'd appeared before. Liam started his hamster impression. He often does when he's asleep. You can always tell when Liam's dreaming because he starts quietly squeaking like a hamster. I'm surrounded by weirdos, I'm telling you.

I must have shut my eyes because something touched my ear and I almost screamed again. There was the alien, only this time I could see that it was actually a girl's head. Obviously the head hadn't come on its own. Presumably there was a body attached, but the rest of her was out of sight. And the reason I'd thought

she was orange was because she had a mass of
ginger curls flaming all over her head like some
Hollywood disaster movie. She grinned at me
and put a finger to her lips.

'Who are you?' I whispered. She waggled her
eyebrows. Great – another weirdo. 'Where did
you come from?' She slowly turned her face
upwards and stared towards the ceiling.

'Up there?' She nodded. 'The next floor up?'
She shook her head. 'Higher?' She nodded
again. 'Top floor?' Shake, shake. 'Above that?'
Nod, nod. 'Above the Earth?' Nod, nod. I
grinned. 'Er, beyond the moon?' Nod, nod,

nod. 'From another planet?' Now she nodded like mad. Then her eyes went all squiffy like a cross-eyed twit and her tongue came out of her mouth, more and more of it, and then, and then . . . her ears waggled.

'OK, now tell me really. Which ward are you on?' The alien looked horrified, and cross too. 'Have I upset you? Because I don't believe you?' She nodded.

'OK, I believe you, you're from another planet, but why don't you speak to me? Why don't you say something?'

She frowned, keeping her eyes on mine, but she wouldn't say anything and her lips were pressed tightly together. She simply carried on staring at me, like her eyes were trying to bore into my brain to see what I was thinking. (What I was thinking was: *This girl's off this planet!*) I gave up.

'OK,' I shrugged. 'Don't speak to me. See if I care.' I gazed around the gloomy ward to show her how much I didn't care. I must have lasted at least five seconds. 'For heaven's sake, say something!' I hissed. But the alien slowly shook her head. 'OK, have it your own way. I'm

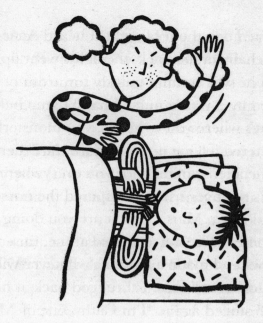

going to guess your name and you nod if I get it
right. Sarah.'

Shake.

'Jasmine?'

Shake.

'Montana?'

Shake. I was already getting fed up. There
must be thousands of girls' names. I could still be
doing this next year. Time to speed things up.

'Fartface – ow!'

I'd been punched by an alien. I was about to
complain when her eyes suddenly widened and

she darted down out of sight. I heard Acne-Man's chair scrape back, the lights went up a bit and he was coming quickly towards my bed, followed by a young nurse I hadn't seen before.

'That's where you've got to, you monster!' he muttered, trying not to disturb the others. 'Cathy's been searching for you everywhere.'

'She's not a monster,' whispered the nurse, smiling. 'Hiya, Maisie. What are you doing down here?' The nurse looked at me, raised her eyebrows and made a kind of 'whatever-will-Maisie-do-next?' face. I shrugged back at her and she smiled again. 'I'm Cathy, one of Maisie's nurses from upstairs. We're supposed to keep an eye on her but sometimes she manages to give us the slip.'

I nodded. She seemed nice, Cathy. She had twinkly eyes and a crinkly smile. Acne-Man stood there with his arms folded, watching.

'She didn't bother you, I hope?' Cathy asked, and I shook my head.

'She gave me a surprise.'

'Yes, she's good at that,' said Cathy.

'We'll never get her out,' complained Acne-Man. 'She's right under the bed.'

Cathy knelt down beside the bed and called softly, 'Come on, Maisie.' The nurse stretched out a hand.

The orange head reappeared almost at once. Maisie's eyes pinpointed Acne-Man and burned. She slipped a hand into Cathy's.

'Night,' laughed Cathy, while Maisie threw a glance back at me, eyes crossed, tongue flapping, and they went padding off.

'Night,' I smiled, while Acne-Man grunted and gazed after them, sighed again and turned his evil eye on me.

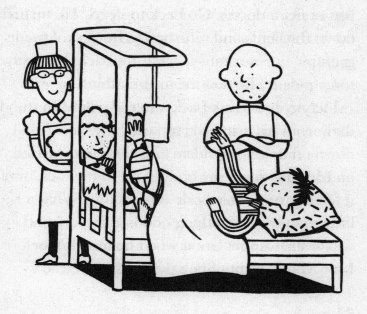

'It would be a good idea if you didn't encourage her,' he suggested.

Urh?! How come it was my fault?

'I've never seen her before in my life. I didn't ask her to come here. She just arrived.'

'Yeah, right, of course she did,' he sneered.

'Who is she, anyway? What's wrong with her?'

Acne-Man stared over towards the door as if the alien was still there. 'Maisie's on the ward above,' he said crossly. 'She's in for observation.'

'Observing what?'

'Just . . . in for observation,' he repeated. 'None of your business. It's doctors' business and you're not a doctor. Go back to sleep.' He turned down the lights and returned to his desk. I made grumpy 'nur-nur-nur' faces at his back. Honestly, some people. Pardon me for breathing.

I let my head sink back into the pillow. In the darkness I felt a smile creep over my face. It slid down on to my shoulders and chest and carried on trickling down my body, right to my toes, until it felt like my whole body was smiling. What a little mystery! Something odd is going on, and whatever it is I'm sure it won't be too long before I see Maisie again. She's definitely a weirdo.

4 How to Demolish a Pyramid

Been awake forever. That's what it feels like.
I must have slept at some point because it's
morning but I don't feel as if I have. It is now
half past five. Half past five! What sort of stupid
time is that? I was OK at first, after Maisie's visit.
I went to sleep all right but something woke me
about four a.m. and my brain started thinking
and once that happened I was wide awake.

I've never liked horror films. I don't like scary
things. But my head kept on replaying this horror
film: *Death in the Supermarket*. I went through it

again and again. There was me, shopping. There was the tomato pyramid. There was the man. Then – disaster. Thunderous banging, a red explosion, like magma from a volcano, relentless.

He didn't have a chance. Helpless horror. I simply stood there aghast and, at the end, buried beneath it all was the body. Everything freezes for a second. A woman screams. People shout and begin to move. Someone rushes forward. I move backward, slowly at first, then a bit faster. Then I'm running. Running away.

Then *ZZZZIIIPPPP*! Play again: There was me shopping. There was the tomato pyramid. There was the man. The man who was going to die . . .

On and on it went. I fought my brain, trying to think of something else, trying to force my mind on to something cheerful and ordinary. Something simple and everyday, like eating supper and plates and knives and forks and *ping*! Do you know what came into my mind? A fork stuck in a bottom.

Why does your mind do things like that? Maybe yours doesn't, but mine does. I just wanted to think of something everyday and what do I get? A fork in my bottom. I'm rather embarrassed to admit that this is something that really happened. I sat on a fork. I did. Not a garden fork – a dinner fork. What an idiot! I mean, what kind of person goes around sticking forks in his bum?

To cut a long story short, the fork was on a chair and I didn't see it and I sat down and then got up again – very, VERY quickly, and with an awful lot of noise, because there was a fork sticking in my backside – my Jackside! Definitely a Jackcident.

It really, really hurt. I tell you, forks are no joke. So, back to the hospital. The nurses were really nice. They didn't laugh because they could see how painful it was. There was blood and everything. And do you know what the nurses said? They said they get lots of injuries like that.

Lots of injuries like forks in bottoms? How stupid can people be? (As stupid as me?!) The prong marks stayed there for weeks. Not that I showed anyone, although I think Mum must have told Mrs Fetlock what had happened because for some while after that, every time I was annoying her she'd fix me with a stare, raise one eyebrow and pat her backside a couple of times. Oh yes, it was pure blackmail – and it worked for a few weeks too.

See what I mean? In the middle of the night,

if you're awake, you end up thinking a load of old rubbish. At least it got my mind off that *Death in the Supermarket* horror film and I must have fallen asleep eventually. The tea lady, Mrs Noseworthy, woke me with a drink and the news that my parents were coming in to see me so the nurse would be in soon to give me a bed bath. That made my day. Lucky me.

I don't suppose it's ever occurred to you to wonder how you do things when you have to lie in bed twenty-four hours a day. You still have to go to the loo and everything. Even Ben worked that one out and he asked all about it when he came in with Mum and Dad on his first visit. Mum and Dad left him with me while they went to get a cup of coffee.

'You have to stay in bed all day?' he asked.

'Yes.'

'How do you go to the toilet then?'

I pointed at the special plastic jug on my bedside table.

'How does that work then?'

'I'm not going to show you!'

'No, but how do you . . . you know?'

'I put it under the covers and pee into it. OK?'

'Wow! Cool! Can I have a go?'

'No.'

Ben picked up the jug and peered into it, frowning. 'What about the other stuff? How do you get that in?' he asked. Ben always liked to get straight to the bottom of things. (I'm going to kill myself in a minute!)

'The nurse brings a bedpan and slips it under me.'

'What does that look like?'

I had to think for a moment. 'The closest I can think of is an unidentified flying object, but smaller, obviously, small enough to fit beneath me.'

'Wow! Cool!'

I gazed at my brother in disbelief. Bedpans were cool? 'You wouldn't say that if you'd ever had to use one,' I answered acidly. At that point Mum and Dad returned from the cafeteria and Ben jumped up excitedly.

'Jack has to use an unidentified flying poo-bowl,' he exclaimed. 'I wish I had one!'

Dad rolled his eyes, groaned and gave me a sad look. 'Honestly, Jack, did you have to tell him things like that?'

Urh? My fault again! Well, SORREEE.

So you can see from that how much fun we have in hospital, and today it was my turn for a bed bath, and all because Mum and Dad were coming in.

'You want to smell nice for your parents, don't you?' asked Tricia, slipping the waterproof sheet between me and the bed. (Tricia's a nurse – come on, keep up! Hospitals are busy places with loads of staff.)

'Why? Are they taking me out to a fancy restaurant?'

'You! You're such a clown.'

'Do I have to have a bath?'

'Yes, you do. Suppose your girlfriend turns up. She won't like you to be all whiffy, will she?'

'I haven't got a girlfriend,' I answered.

'What about Maisie? She's taken a shine to you.'

That was news to me. 'How do you know?' I asked. 'I thought she didn't speak to anyone.'

'That's right, but she writes things down and shows them to Cathy or me.'

'I don't know why she likes me,' I murmured.

'Neither do I,' laughed Tricia. 'Anyhow, Cathy's bringing her down later. She wants to see you. There, all done. My, you do smell sweet!'

'Yuk,' I said.

Sure enough, an hour later Cathy and Maisie turned up. Cathy left Maisie with Tricia and came across to have a word. She explained that Maisie didn't speak and they didn't know why, but for some reason she seemed to have taken a liking to me.

'So I thought it might be a good idea if I brought her down so she didn't have to sneak off and I knew where she was. She'd just like to sit near you. Is that OK?'

'I'm not going anywhere.'

'It might be your sense of humour she likes,' laughed Cathy. 'I'll go and fetch her.'

Maisie came and sat on the chair next to my bed.

'I shall leave you two to natter,' said Cathy. 'If you want me, I'll be over at the desk.'

Natter? How do you natter with someone who won't speak? What's the point in talking to someone who doesn't answer? Maisie sat there. I lay there. There was a long silence. I tried to think of something to say.

'They think you're my girlfriend,' I said coldly.

Maisie's face broke into a grin. She even squeaked a sniggery sort of squeak. I clasped my hands behind my head and glanced at her.

'I don't think we should marry,' I said seriously. 'Not yet. I think we should wait until . . . until I'm old enough, until I'm about . . . three hundred and fifty.'

This time she doubled up and gave a great snort of laughter. It was good when she laughed. Obviously she could make *some* noises and that cheered me up.

'How old are you?' I asked. Maisie held up her hands.

'Nine? I'm eleven. My parents are coming in later. I had to have a bed bath because of them coming in. I hate bed baths, do you?' Maisie didn't seem to know what a bed bath was. 'Right,

of course, you can bath yourself, can't you? I'm stuck in this bed with my leg. I'm not allowed to move. So the nurse baths me, in bed.' I nodded across at Cathy. Maisie grinned and bit her lower lip. Obviously she didn't fancy a bed bath any more than I did. 'Do your mum and dad come to see you?'

Maisie shook her head. She seemed cross and gazed at the floor. 'Don't they come in at all?' I asked, but she wouldn't look at me. I thought I'd better change the subject. 'I broke my leg, the top bone. I've got to stay here for ages before I'm allowed up. I have to stay on my back all day long and I'm hacked off. Been here four weeks already so I might be able to get up soon.'

Maisie stopped staring at the floor. She reached over, touched my leg gently and looked at me enquiringly. 'You want to know how it happened?' She nodded and I began to tell her and before I knew it I was telling her everything, the whole *Death in the Supermarket* scenario. Maybe I felt safe because she couldn't speak. Maybe that was why. Whatever, I told her everything.

'Mum sent me to get some milk from the supermarket. I went on my bike – twenty-seven gears,' I added proudly and Maisie shrugged. 'You don't know about mountain bikes?' I sighed. 'Never mind. In the supermarket there was a special display, a big pyramid of tomato tins, right up to the ceiling. Absolutely gigantic. There must have been at least a thousand tins, two, three thousand. I bet they were up all night building that. Must have taken them hours. They'd done it for a competition. GUESS HOW MANY TINS IN OUR TOMATO PYRAMID AND WIN A TRIP TO ITALY. Something like that.'

I took a deep breath. Maisie was listening intently. I leaned even closer and lowered my voice. 'The thing is . . . the thing is . . .' I swallowed a couple of times. 'I think my basket . . . well, I'm a bit clumsy. I'm always having accidents and my basket must have caught the edge of the pyramid, or maybe it was my foot.'

Maisie's eyes bulged as she fixed them on me. I gave a little nod. 'There was an old man. He was standing next to the pyramid, reading a competition leaflet and trying to count the tins. Anyhow, I must have clipped the edge of the pyramid and it toppled over. The whole thing, thousands of tins of tomatoes. They came crashing down. It was horrible! I leaped back, tins tumbling everywhere, and when I looked

where the pyramid had been there was just an
enormous pile of tins and . . . and . . .'

I dropped my voice to an almost silent whisper.
'There was a mountain of tins and right at
the bottom, underneath everything, was a pair
of legs – just, just his feet – and they weren't
moving.'

Maisie slowly took her hand away from her
mouth. It had fallen open. The colour had
drained from her face, her eyes wide with alarm.

'Bedpans!' she said.

5 How to Make a Promise, Maisie-style

'What?' I was gobsmacked.

'Bedpans. Cathy won't let me swear, so I say "bedpans" instead.'

I clapped my hands over my head in desperation. 'But hang on, you can't speak!'

'Of course I can. I just did, didn't I?'

'Yeah, but I mean, you don't.'

Maisie rolled her eyes in mock despair. 'That's not the same as *can't*. *Don't* is different. *Don't* means I choose not to.'

'All right, all right, so you can speak, but you don't. Now all of sudden you are. OK, I've got that bit straight in my head, but what's this about bedpans? I mean, none of us are supposed to swear, so we don't, but you say "bedpans" when you want to swear, even though nobody can hear you because you're not actually speaking out loud, you're only saying it in your head?'

Maisie was grinning and nodding.

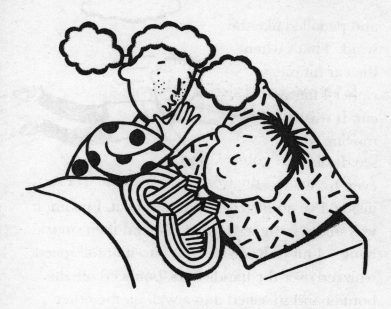

'They can't hear you!' I spluttered.

Maisie leaned towards me and dropped her voice. 'They might hear my thoughts,' she whispered. I heaved a sigh and looked at her sadly.

'You're mad,' I told her.

'So? You've left three thousand tins of tomatoes piled on top of an old man. What happened? Was he all right?'

Her words threw me back into the horror film. I shook my head.

'It was awful. I ran for it, grabbed my bike

and pedalled like the wind. That's when the car hit me, or rather I hit the car. It wasn't moving, you see. It didn't even have anyone inside! I've no idea why I didn't see it. I mean, it was smack bang in front of me and then smack bang – I hit it. Rode straight into it at full speed, whizzed over the handlebars, bounced off the bonnet and smashed into a wall on the other side. That's how I broke my leg. So everyone thinks I fell off my mountain bike and I did. But they don't know why. They never asked. So I've never told anyone. Except you.'

Maisie had been holding her breath all that time. Now she sat back in her chair and slowly let it out. 'Bedpans! Was he . . . was he dead?'

I looked at her. It was too dreadful for words. 'It's a secret,' I whispered. 'The police are bound to come looking for me sooner or later. They'll ask a few questions, put two and two together and any day now they'll come walking through that door with a warrant for my arrest. You've got to keep it to yourself. Don't tell anyone.'

Maisie nodded. She reached out, put both her hands on one of mine, looked me in the eye very seriously and said: 'Cross my heart or die from a fart.'

Excuse me? Had I heard that correctly? 'What? I thought it was "Cross my heart and hope to die". That's not what we say at school.'

'I don't go to your school,' Maisie pointed out. 'We say "Cross my heart or die from a fart". At least I do, and you'd better not let on about me talking, either, because that's *my* secret.'

'Cross my heart,' I began, but never actually finished because at that point two people arrived at the door.

'Is that the police?' whispered Maisie.

'No, my parents.'

Mum and Dad came across, beaming at me, and Mum leaned over and gave me a kiss, which was embarrassing, but inescapable if you've got a broken leg. She smiled at Maisie.

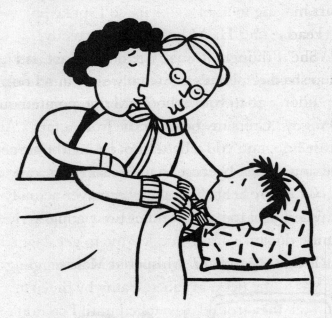

'Hello, what's your name?' My heart sank but Maisie silently smiled back. 'Do you have a name?' prompted Mum and then, because Maisie remained quiet, Mum suddenly put a hand to her mouth. 'Oh, I'm so sorry! You're deaf, aren't you? Can you lip-read?'

Before I could stop her Mum bent down very close to Maisie, pointed at her mouth with both hands and said 'S-O-R-R-Y,' making her lips move very slowly. I couldn't stand it any longer. Mum was making a clown of herself and Maisie was making fools of all of us, so I spoke up instead.

'She's Maisie and she's not deaf, Mum. It's just that she doesn't speak. Actually, she comes from another planet. She's here under observation and she's completely poo-brained.'

'Jack!' snapped Dad. 'That's enough. Don't be so unkind.' He turned to Maisie. 'I'm sorry about our son. He can be very rude.'

Maisie got to her feet. She threw a highly amused glance at me and left me to get slagged off by my own parents while she went giggling across to the desk, grabbed Cathy by the arm and off they trotted. I watched until I couldn't see them any longer, wondering if my secret would be safe with the ginger alien.

Mum and Dad had brought some photos of Lazybones, my cat. He's black and white, purrs like a Harley-Davidson and likes to lie across my shoulders when I'm watching telly. 'He misses you,' said Dad. 'So does Ben. He's over at his friend's place today – we thought it might be more peaceful to visit without him.'

'We all miss you,' said Mum, stroking my hair. Princess La-La sniggered at me from across the room. She mouthed the words 'mummy's boy' at me. I hurriedly pulled my head away.

'I'll be home soon,' I murmured hopefully.

'Of course you will,' said Mum. 'Doctor says you're making excellent progress.' She sniffed the air. 'You smell of hospital soap.'

'They gave me a bed bath this morning,' I muttered darkly. 'I am considering writing to ChildLine. My human rights have been violated.'

'Darling, if you don't wash regularly you will become a stink bomb, and then everybody else will feel that their human rights have been violated by you.' Mum smiled triumphantly, as if she'd outsmarted me, which I guess she had, sort of, again.

'We could have a party when you come out,' Dad suggested, and I know he meant come out of hospital, but to me it sounded like come out of prison.

'You could invite Daisy,' Mum said. 'That

would be nice. She'd like that.'

'Her name's Maisie, and what's the point of inviting someone who's not going to talk to anyone?'

'It's not her fault, poor thing,' said Mum.

And I thought to myself: *Yes, it is. She does it on purpose. But why?*

Mum and Dad stayed for about two hours and it wasn't until after they'd gone that I was able to put my brain to good use. Princess La-La had been smirking at me all the time my parents stayed, so I started to think of a way to get even with her and eventually I came up with a plan. My big problem was that I was stuck in bed, so I needed someone to help. I called Liam over and explained my idea.

'Cool!' he said. 'Where's the note?'

I scribbled a quick message.

> **Darling Ashley,**
> **You are cute.**
> **I fancy you.**
> **K.**

'That should do it,' I said, folding it in half.

'Wicked!' Liam slipped the note into his pocket.

'You know what to do,' I said.

'Just watch me,' he answered. He sauntered back to his bed, making a bit of a detour to get to Acne-Man's desk and slipping the note on it while he wasn't there. Liam turned and gave me a broad wink. He was good at winking, I'll say that for him.

I didn't feel any better about things though and the day dragged on. It was one of those days, a real draggy day – do you know what I mean? Telling Maisie about the supermarket had left me feeling flat and empty. All I could be bothered to do was stare at the ceiling, the walls and . . . the doors. The Doors of Doom. I had never known such threatening doors. Every time they banged open my heart stopped because I knew, I *knew* that sooner or later the police would walk in and the game would be up.

They say that sometimes in cop stories on TV, don't they? 'The game's up! You're nicked, son!' But it's not a game at all. Games are supposed to be fun and I can tell you that waiting for the

police to come and get you is no fun
at all.

And then the Doors of Doom did
bang and my heart missed a beat,
clocked who it was and started again.

Great, here comes Miss Crispin, from
the hospital school. Lucky me.

Oh yes, we even have school in hospital. There
is no escaping school or baths. Miss Crispin
had a project for me to do. Maths. My favourite
subject. (That's called irony. Mrs Fetlock taught
me that. At first I thought it must have something
to with actual ironing, but it doesn't.)

'I want you to make a bar chart,' said Miss
Crispin. 'It can be about anything you like. For
example, how many different kinds of
people come into this ward
during the day.'

'Different kinds? Like
how many people with only
one eye? How many with
heads stuck in saucepans?
How many with broken –'

'No, Jack, that isn't what
I mean. How many men,

women, boys, girls, nurses, parents and so on come walking through those doors? That's what I mean.'

Bedpans – as a certain person might say. The Doors of Doom again. And a maths project. What a lovely day I was having. My happiness was complete.

6 How Not to Score a Goal

I've told you how I'm always having accidents.
Today's example – spilled my breakfast all down
my front. Princess La-La jeered and told Tricia
I needed a bib. She doesn't know about the
note yet. I'm sure Acne-Man keeps giving her
funny looks. Anyway, bar charts. There must be
something interesting I could think up. Maybe
I could do something about all my Jackcidents.
How many times have I banged my head?
(Loads!) How many times have I hurt my knee?
(Lots!)

There was one really cracking accident I
had when I did both knees in at the same time
playing five-a-side football on the school's
AstroTurf pitch. I was racing about, thinking
how fantabulous it would be to actually score and
all at once I had the ball at my feet and the goal
was right in front and everyone was shouting and
yelling, and my foot smashed into the ball. Away

it soared and the goalkeeper jumped and his arms went up and the ball whizzed straight over his hands and into the net. Brilliantissimo! I had scored! Me! Jack! Scored!

I turned and ran back down the pitch and I did The Slide. You know, when you score and you throw yourself down on your knees and you slide across the grass. Wonderful!

Unless it's AstroTurf. If it's AstroTurf it isn't like sliding on grass. It's like sliding across a cheese grater. It took all the skin off my knees. Talk about OW!

But it was worse than that even. I thought everyone was cheering when I scored that goal, but they weren't. They were bellowing at me to stop. I had been racing up and down the pitch so much I'd clean forgotten which way I was kicking and I'd scored in my own goal!

But remembering that did get me thinking about the bits of the body that get the worst of it. Which bits do you think get hit most? Head? Elbows? Knees? Bum? Maybe I should do a bar chart about that. I'll think about it.

I was still thinking about it when the doc came round the ward checking the charts that hang on the ends of our beds and generally making sure we were still breathing and hadn't died. He looked me up and down and narrowed his eyes.

He's got bad news, I thought. He always narrows his eyes when he's got bad news. 'You must be pretty fed up with being stuck in a hospital bed,' he began. 'So as of today you can start sitting up and tomorrow we're going to get you on your feet.'

I almost leaped up there and then. 'Really?'

He gave me a broad smile. 'Thought that might cheer you up. Your leg's doing pretty well

and I think it's time we got it moving properly
– a bit of gentle exercise. I'll speak to physio and
get it set up. They'll show you what you can do
and what you should avoid for a while. A few
days' practice, then you can go home.'

Home! Was that music to my ears? It was like
a big brass band trumpeting all the way down
the hospital corridors. TA TARA-TA TA! Jack
Lemming can get up! PAR-PARA-PAH PAH!
Jack Lemming – you can go home! PISH! (The
'PISH!' bit was the big cymbals.)

As soon as the doc had gone I announced the news to the whole ward. Ashley came across and performed the Grand Ceremony of the Sitting Up. My pillows are on a frame that can be tilted at different angles. He has to set it for me at the moment, but at least I can sit up and see more.

Liam seemed pretty chirpy as well. 'I'm going home too,' he said. Princess La-La turned her back on the pair of us and I guessed she was staying. I wished she'd smile sometimes.

'Uh-oh,' said Liam. 'Watch out, here comes your Little Miss Weirdo. Don't know what you see in her. She doesn't even talk.'

'Makes her a good listener,' I explained, watching Maisie skip into the ward with Cathy. 'I can say stuff to her that I might not say to anyone else.'

'Weirdo,' Liam repeated before darting off to his bed-cave.

Cathy and Maisie came straight across. 'She wanted to come and see you,' said Cathy. 'Don't ask me why.'

Maisie's eyes sparkled. She settled in the chair beside me while Cathy watched. 'She likes coming to see you, so what do you talk to her about?'

I shrugged.

'Hmm, secrets, I suppose.'

I shrugged again and Cathy laughed. 'My, my, that's two of you not talking. I'd better go away in case it spreads even further and we have an epidemic of silence throughout the hospital. OK, I don't mind. I'll go and talk to Ashley. Have fun!' As she crossed the ward Acne-Man beckoned her over. They kept laughing and snatching glances. Very odd.

'She fancies him,' whispered Maisie, as if she'd read my mind.

'Urgh! How could anyone fancy Acne-Man?'

'Doesn't matter. It'll end in tears anyway. Always does.'

'How do you mean?'

'People never stay together,' she said simply. 'They always split up.'

'My parents haven't split up.'

'I bet they will.'

'Don't say that! What would you know, anyway?'

'They always do. None of my friends have got both parents. Some have got two dads and some have got two mums and some have only got a

dad or a mum, except Sophie, and she's got three
dads – one proper and two stepdads.'

'Well, my parents aren't going to split up,' I
said staunchly.

'They won't bother to ask *you*,' snorted Maisie.
'Don't be so stupid.'

'I'm not stupid!'

'Keep your voice down. I don't want anyone to
hear.'

'Oh, right? Why not? And don't say "because".
Why can't anyone hear what Little Miss
Smartypants Alien has to say?'

Maisie scowled back. 'You won't tell?'

'Cross my heart or die from a fart. OK?'

'My dad's gone – a few months ago. One day
he was there and the next day he wasn't. Neither
of them said a word. They never told me. So
now I'm not telling them anything either. I don't
speak to Mum. Haven't spoken to her for ages.'

'You're crazy!'

'Not.'

'Are. How long have you been keeping that
up?'

'Seven months. Mum thinks there's something
wrong with me and that's why I'm here. They
keep trying to get me to speak, but I won't.'

'You can't *not* speak forever.'

'Can if I want.' Maisie sulked for a bit.
'Anyway,' she eventually murmured, 'it's gone on
so long I can't just start again. If Mum knows I
could have spoken all this time she'll be furious.'

'No, she won't.'

'Will. When my mum's cross she's like a tiger
on fire.'

'A tiger on fire?' I repeated, puzzled.

'You'd be cross if you were a tiger and you
were on fire, wouldn't you?' said Maisie. 'And

tigers are dangerous, so a tiger on fire would be really, REALLY dangerous. Stop laughing, it's not funny.'

I tried to look serious. 'Are you going to stay silent for the rest of your life?'

'No, stupid, only until I'm eighteen and then I can leave home.'

'Eighteen! Maisie, that's – um, ten, nine years from now! You're mad.'

'And you can get stuffed!' she swore. She jumped up, flounced across the ward, grabbed a very surprised Cathy from the desk and dragged her from the room.

'Get stuffed yourself,' I muttered. But she'd gone. Girls – they're always trouble.

I didn't have much time to think about it though, because shortly after that Acne-Man came over with some news.

'There's a visitor for you tomorrow. A man phoned and asked if it would be all right and I said yes, you wouldn't be going anywhere.' He grinned at me and went on. 'He seemed to think it was important and he needed to speak to you. He's an inspector, he said. Probably going to arrest you.'

Looking at Acne-Man's face I could see he thought he was making a joke. Some joke! I could only nod. My mouth had gone totally dry. I was numb from my toes to the tips of the hair on my head. This was it. Tomorrow was going to be Doomsday and there was nothing I could do and nowhere to run, because I had a broken leg and couldn't run at all. There was no escape. I wondered if there'd be handcuffs.

7 How to Escape from Hospital

Three o'clock in the morning – do you think
I could sleep? No way. Kirsty's been talking in
hers. She does different voices as if she's having a
conversation with herself! She had a deep gruff
voice that said: '. . . get down!' Then Kirsty's
normal voice whimpered: 'But I'm only a little
squirrel.' What with that AND Liam doing his
hamster impressions it's no wonder I was awake.

I wished it was me fast asleep, dreaming
about squirrels. Instead of which I was having
a waking nightmare. The police were coming
in the morning and I was scared. I felt so alone
– except I wasn't.

'Pssst!'

'Maisie?'

'Yes.'

'What are you doing here?'

'Couldn't sleep.'

'Me neither. Why couldn't you sleep?'

'My eyes were open.'

I had to put a hand over my mouth to stifle a snort. 'You're crazy.'

'Stop saying that. I'm not. You're horrid.'

'Sorry. I'm just . . . well, the police are coming to see me tomorrow.'

'Bedpans!'

'Exactly.' I paused for a moment and added quietly, 'I'm scared, Maisie. Someone died and it was my fault and now they're going to question me and I'll have to go to court and I'll end up in jail.'

'You could escape!' Maisie said eagerly. 'I'll help you. We'll tie your sheets together, you climb out of the window, slide down and disappear into the night.'

'I've got a broken leg and five kilos of sand hanging from my foot. I don't think I'll get very far.'

'Wimp,' she muttered before sinking into thought. 'All right, what about this? You pretend to be dead. They'll have to take you from the ward then. How long can you hold your breath for?'

'I don't know.'

'Hold it now and I'll time you. Ready? Go.'
Maisie began counting. She only got as far as
seventeen and then I had to breathe again.

'I don't think that's going to be long enough,' I
said dolefully and Maisie nodded.

'Seventeen isn't very long. I can hold mine
for fifty. Watch.' She took a huge breath
and then counted at breakneck speed.
'Fortysevenfortyeightfortynine – fifty!'

'Yeah, but you counted much faster for you.'

'That's because I'm smaller and younger.'

'What difference does that make?'

'My dad said – before he LEFT ME – he said that as you get older and bigger you do things more slowly, so I was counting more slowly for you.'

I shook my head. 'You've completely lost me now. I haven't a clue what you're talking about.'

'Well, I don't know what my dad was talking about either,' Maisie shot back. 'He and Mum just used to say stuff and I never knew what half of it meant.' She was right there. My parents were a bit like that. Still are.

'Look, don't worry,' she went on. 'Just make sure you don't breathe when they look at you. Then they'll wheel you away.'

'Where?' I asked cautiously.

'Um, well, this is a hospital so there must be people dying sometimes. I bet they have a big fire somewhere and they'll put you on it.'

'Maisie! That's horrible!'

'That's what they do with dead bodies. Anyway, you don't have to stay on it,' Maisie said quickly. 'You could jump up and run away . . .'

'. . . with my broken leg,' I reminded her.

'You're just making excuses, you and your stupid broken leg.' She lapsed into silence once more. Then I began to chuckle. I couldn't help it.

'What?' asked Maisie.

'Put me on a bonfire! That is so crazy!'

She grinned back at me, but it wasn't long before I felt the smile fade from my face. My voice sank to a whisper of a whisper. 'I'm really, really scared,' I murmured.

'How do you know someone died?' Maisie asked.

'I saw his feet, remember? And he wasn't moving.'

'Maybe he was sleeping,' she suggested.

'I don't think it's very likely, not with fifty thousand tins of tomatoes on top of him.'

'He could have been unconscious. Anyhow, you don't know for sure he was dead.'

'He wasn't moving,' I repeated. 'People were yelling. Someone was shouting for an ambulance.'

Maisie suddenly gripped my arm. 'He would have been brought here, to the hospital,' she whispered.

'Probably. So?'

'We could investigate, like detectives. We could find out what happened to him. Don't worry, I'll think of something. I am going to save you.'

Great. Maisie the Weird Alien was going to come to my rescue. But even as I heaved a sigh I began to think she might be on to something. Maybe I *should* try and find out a bit more. I'd knocked the tins over and there was definitely a body beneath them, but *was he dead*? I'd have to ask questions around the hospital. How could I do that without arousing suspicion?

That was when a big, bright light went on in my brain. Of course! Miss Crispin's Maths project. I could do a bar chart about injuries like I'd been thinking of, *except that the injuries wouldn't be mine – they'd be other people's injuries!* Suppose I

did a chart for different kinds of injuries and
illnesses in the hospital on different days? I could
ask staff if there'd been any crush injuries on the
day of my accident. At least it would be a start. I
turned to Maisie.

'Listen, suppose we . . . Maisie?'

She'd gone.

8 How to Make an Entrance

I must have slept after that because the next
thing I remember was Mrs Noseworthy shouting
in my ear.

'Tea or coffee?' she yelled.

'Nothing.'

'I haven't got any nothing, young man. You've
got to get up your strength. Won't be long before
you're out of here. Got to feed those muscles in
your leg.'

'Squash then,' I growled.

'That's better,' said Mrs Noseworthy. 'You're
looking peaky this morning. I'll be back later. I'll
see if I can get you some biscuits. That'll put a
smile on your face.'

I almost died of shock. Mrs Noseworthy was
being nice to me! Amazing! And then of course
I realized why. It was because the police were
coming to arrest me. She only felt sorry for
me, that's all. I expect the whole hospital knew

by now. The police were coming for Jack, the
eleven-year-old criminal. The killer.

'Can you help me sit up?' I asked Mrs
Noseworthy, and she adjusted the bed. Liam gave
me a thumbs up and pointed across to the desk. I
was surprised to see Cathy there, talking to Acne-
Man, who had just come on duty for the day.
They were smiling at each other and touching
hands. Very strange.

Liam slipped from his bed and came over. 'I
saw them snogging,' he said excitedly.

'You never did! What – I mean, like real . . .?'
Urgh. It was almost too disgusting to consider.

'And I heard what they were saying,' he continued. 'Acne-Man said he'd always fancied her . . .'

'Yuk!'

'. . . and he said he didn't have the courage to say anything about it until he got the note she wrote.'

'She was writing him notes?'

'No, she wasn't,' grinned Liam. 'Cathy was really surprised and asked him what note was he talking about and he said the note she left on his desk.'

It took a few seconds for the penny to drop.
And then I got it. 'You mean the note I . . . the
one you . . .?'

Liam nodded.

'But it was from Kirsty, K for Kirsty. I didn't
put Cathy.'

'I know, but it's Kathy with a K,
not Cathy with a C, see?'

'Oh, bummy bums!' I cried.

'Now look what you've started,'
Liam said. 'It's disgusting.'

It might have been disgusting but I was a bit
miffed. It had been a perfect plan and it had
failed.

'Rats,' I hissed, and at exactly the same
moment had an utterly brilliant idea. 'Quick, nip
across to Kirsty's bed while she's snoozing and
grab her chart.'

'Why?'

'Just do it, before anyone sees.'

Liam slipped over, took the chart off the end
of Kirsty's bed and brought it back. I took my
pen and quickly added a steep upward line to
Kirsty's temperature. 'Put it back, quick.'

Liam had only just managed to get the chart

back in place and himself in bed when the ward door swung open and my blood froze. A tall, sharp man came in, glancing round the room, his hard eyes glittering like tiny stones. He marched across to the desk lugging a large, heavy briefcase with him. It obviously had something important inside, like a portable torture rack.

'I'm here to interview Jack Lemming,' he announced loudly, and my heart went into a steep nosedive. My face was burning. I could feel everyone's eyes on me. I hardly dared look at the man as he approached, and then I saw my parents arrive. I didn't know whether to be glad or worried. Thank goodness they were here, but then they'd find out about everything!

I closed my eyes and wished I was far away on a desert island somewhere, just me all by myself on a warm beach with some coconuts and a tinkling waterfall nearby with sparkly fresh water and lots of free food and a pet monkey to play with and a boat – a cabin cruiser with twin outboard motors and some . . .

'Jack?'

I opened my eyes. I wasn't on a warm beach. I was still in a hospital bed. I started to sweat.

'Yes.'

'Hi, Jack,' smiled Dad. 'We came in because the inspector needs to ask you some questions about your accident. It's quite straightforward.'

Oh, Dad! If only it was straightforward! But it wasn't. It was the opposite. What is the opposite of straightforward? Bentbackward. That'd be it. It was all bentbackward.

'Perhaps I could ask a few questions?' suggested the inspector, his cold eyes resting on mine. 'I'm Mr Cutter. Managed to track you down at last. I was beginning to think you'd gone into hiding. I need to ask you some questions about the day of the accident. You were at the supermarket?'

I nodded and gritted my teeth. Beads of sweat broke out on my forehead.

'You left the supermarket on your bike and you rode into a car?'

'Yes,' I croaked.

'What colour was the car?'

My mind was being sucked into a whirlpool. What colour was the car? What on earth did he want to know that for? It must be a trick. He was trying to unsettle me and force me into a

confession. I thought rapidly. Well, I'd got clever
Mr Cutter sussed. He wasn't going to get the
better of me!

'It was black,' I said. (Which was true-ish. The
tyres were black. In detective stories they call this

'laying a false trail'. In other words I was leading
Inspector Cutter right up the garden path.)

Ha! You should have seen the effect that had!
Cutter's eyebrows slid right the way up his head
and stayed there for at least ten seconds. I bet I
could fool Sherlock Holmes if I wanted. 'Black?'
repeated Mr Cutter.

'Yes.'

'It wasn't . . . red?'

'Yes,' I agreed. 'It was red, and black. With silver bits.'

Mr Cutter turned to Mum and Dad. 'Just making sure we've got the right vehicle.' He looked a bit perplexed. 'Is your son always like this?'

'What do you mean?' asked Mum.

'Is he always . . .' Mr Cutter struggled for a word. 'Odd?' he suggested, and Mum and Dad both nodded vigorously.

'Oh yes. He's always been very odd,' said Mum. 'But he did fall on his head when he was three.'

'And again when he was five,' added Dad.

'And five and a half,' Mum threw in for good measure. Thanks a bundle, Mum, Dad. You're real pals.

Mr Cutter frowned. 'Tell me, Jack, what was the *main* colour of the car?'

'Um, red? I think.'

He wrote that down. 'And the car was moving?'

'No. It was parked.'

'Was anyone inside?' I shook my head. 'You crashed into an empty parked car that wasn't moving?'

'Yes.'

'Why? I mean how come you didn't see a parked car right in front of you?'

'My eyes were half shut.'

'Oh, Jack,' sighed Mum.

'He's a bit of a lemon,' Dad explained, a trifle crossly.

'Just for the record, why were your eyes half shut?'

'It's to stop bees and midges and things getting into them when I'm riding fast.'

'Does that happen often?'

'No, because I keep them half shut.' I was thinking: *this man's an idiot! Does he think I do this for fun?* Dad was giving me dark scowls for some reason. Mr Cutter tapped his pen thoughtfully on his notepad.

'Yes, of course. So you were riding fast? Why was that?'

Bums! My false trail hadn't worked. I bit my lower lip. This was it. They'd all find out any second now.

82

'Anyone for tea?'

Phew! It was Mrs Noseworthy with the tea trolley. I'd never been so pleased to see her. She stood there with one hand holding the big metal teapot and the other on her trolley. And then, and then . . .

. . . AND THEN – the curtain round the side of the trolley slowly fell open and a body tumbled out and crumpled on to the floor beside my bed. It lay there, face up, arms and legs

spreadeagled, with a huge red bloodstain across
the chest.

It was Maisie, the ginger alien.

For a tiny moment all you could hear was the
dribble and splash of tea pouring out of Mrs
Noseworthy's teapot and on to the floor and her
long, reverse scream, as if she was swallowing it.
Her mouth was as wide as the Channel Tunnel
and instead of the scream coming out of her
mouth it was being sucked back in.

The teapot fell to the floor with a clatter and
a moment later Mrs Noseworthy followed. Her
legs seemed to fold up beneath her and she
collapsed in a heap, right in the middle of the
tea-puddle.

'Oh, my . . .' began the inspector, then his eyes
seemed to disappear inside his skull. He toppled
forward and sprawled across Mrs Noseworthy
while Mum and Dad just stood there, gazing
down at the ever-increasing pile of bodies at
their feet.

Acne-Man and Tricia came hurtling across.
Tricia plunged on to her knees beside Maisie
and just as she bent over her, the dead Maisie
suddenly sat up! She gave everyone a manic grin,

flung her arms wide and cried out: 'Yippee! I'm alive! I can speak!' Then up she jumped and began to stride round the ward. 'I can walk! I can talk! It's a miracle!'

And it was, sort of.

9 How I Start Investigating

Complete chaos. Mrs Noseworthy had to be given oxygen and then she went and had a sit-down in the restroom for half an hour. Mr Cutter was lifted on to a stretcher and carted away. Mum and Dad sat on my bed looking totally confused, and who could blame them?

But it was Maisie who was the focus of attention. Acne-Man couldn't believe his ears. He grabbed Maisie and shouted at her. 'Can you really talk?'

'Yes!'

'Blimey!' said Acne-Man. 'Er, wait. I'll have to test you, see if your brain's all right. Er, how many fingers am I holding up?'

'Three!'

'Blimey!' said Acne-Man. 'Er, what's the capital of Rome?'

'Rome *is* a capital,' answered Maisie. 'The capital of Italy.'

'Blimey!' said Acne-Man. 'Er, why is there
blood all over your front?'

'It's tomato sauce,' Maisie giggled.

'Blimey!' said Acne-Man. 'She can talk!' he
announced, in case we hadn't noticed.

Maisie stood there, surrounded by amazed
hospital staff, while Kathy smiled like it was
Christmas Day and she'd just opened her best
present.

'I was wondering where you'd got to, you little
tinker.'

'I'm not a tinker, I'm a talker,' replied Maisie
coolly.

'So I see. And how come you can talk all of a sudden?'

'Jack taught me,' she said. Everyone swivelled round and looked at me. What could I do? I was just as surprised as everyone else.

Kathy smiled. 'Thank you, Jack. I knew there was something going on between you.'

'No, there isn't. She's not my girlfriend!' I blurted.

'But you're *his* girlfriend,' sniggered Maisie, pointing at Acne-Man, who turned into a beetroot on the spot, while Kathy blushed a delicate pink. She took Maisie by the hand.

'We'd better go back upstairs. I think we have some exciting news for your mother.'

The smile slipped from Maisie's face. As they left the ward Maisie turned round and glanced back at me. I gave her a thumbs-up sign. She pressed her lips together determinedly and then

they'd gone.

Mum and Dad stayed on for ages, while a cleaner came in and mopped up the spilled tea and the big blobs of tomato sauce that Maisie had somehow managed to spread round the entire ward. It even had her footprints in it. My parents wanted to know everything about Maisie. Mum shook her head sadly. 'Strange girl. How can she be cured? Doesn't she know she's deaf?'

'Sometimes you have no idea what goes on in their heads,' said Dad, and for a moment I didn't know whether he was talking about Maisie or Mum. 'Why did she pretend to be dead?'

I knew the answer to that one. 'Dad, you have to remember that Maisie is a creature from another universe.'

'Right,' murmured Dad. 'That would explain it, I suppose.'

I was expecting Mr Cutter to return and interrogate me again but he didn't, which was only half a relief. He was bound to come back sooner or later, dragging his torture rack with him. It was just a matter of time. There must be something I could do before he returned – maybe find out something.

Long after my parents had gone Maisie reappeared with Kathy, who went straight across to Acne-Man of course.

'Do you think they'll get married?' I asked Maisie. She shrugged.

'Who knows? What did you think of my miracle?'

'Cool!'

'I thought if I could make something astonishing happen it would make that policeman go away, and it did.'

'He'll be back,' I added gloomily. 'And if it's not him it will be a different one. They're all after me.'

'But you might be innocent. Somebody might have set you up because they have a grudge against you. They do that in movies.'

'This is real life, Maisie. I've been thinking about the dead body. We could try and find out more.'

'Like an autopsy!' said Maisie. 'They do that on telly, in murder mysteries. They open up the dead body to find out how they were murdered.'

'Yeah, I've seen it on telly too. Gruesome.'

'Great!' beamed Maisie. 'I'd love to do that. I'd cut open the body and say – goodness me,

Sergeant Lemming, this man was stabbed to death with a drawing pin!'

'You're mad,' I chuckled. 'Anyway, if you opened up the man under the pyramid you'd only find tomato tins.' I was trying to be funny, but it didn't sound the least bit comical really. Not to me. I went on.

'I thought I could go down to Casualty tomorrow and ask a few questions. I've got this daft bar chart to do for Miss Crispin. I could pretend I want to know about accidents and stuff.'

'And I could help,' said Maisie, putting on her 'intelligent and helpful' face – the one that made her look like a very confused mouse stuck in a maze.

'I guess,' I answered doubtfully. 'What did your mum say when she discovered you can speak after all?'

Maisie gave a hoot of laughter. 'She was so astonished *she* couldn't speak!' Her face became serious. 'Then she cried and hugged me. I almost stopped breathing. I kept thinking all her tears are going to make a huge puddle and it'll come through the ceiling and crash down on Jack and

it'll probably drown him and kill him and if it
doesn't do that all the falling plaster will probably
break his other leg.'

'You're daft.'

'Not as stupid as you. Anyway, she cried lots
and said she'd felt so alone and it was like she'd
lost Dad AND she'd lost me because I wasn't
speaking.'

There was a short silence. Maisie stared at me
hard and her eyes went sort of shimmery and
she stared at her feet instead. 'When she told
me that it made me cry too,' Maisie said with

a deep sigh. I hate it when people cry. I never know what to do, so I just kept quiet until Maisie suddenly lifted her head, sniffed and grinned at me. 'And I'm not telling you any more because it's P – R – I – V – A – T – E between me and Mum. Anyhow, I can go home now.'

Oof! That was a blow. I was surprised how I felt about that, like the breath had been knocked out of me. It wasn't as if we were fantastic buddies or anything – she's nine and I'm eleven. But she'd been fun and she'd saved me from Mr Cutter and stopped me dying of boredom and – oh, all sorts of things. Liam was going, and now Maisie. I was going to be on my own – apart from Princess La-La, who was about as much fun as a used tissue.

'But I have to come back tomorrow for some tests so I'll see you then and I can help you do that investigating.'

Hmmm. I got that sinking sensation in my stomach – a feeling of fast-approaching doom. Somehow the words 'Maisie', 'help' and 'investigating' weren't nearly as encouraging as she meant them to be.

10 How Not to Conduct an Investigation

I'm up! I can walk – almost.
Actually, it feels more like
my leg has turned into
a log and I'm hauling
a large bit of tree trunk
around. Paul – he's the
physio – he says I'll
soon get used to it.

'My mum
said that about
Christmas cake,' I
told him. 'And I still
can't stand the stuff.'

'I think you'll find a
broken leg is a bit different
from Christmas cake,' he
answered. He's given me
lots of exercises to do to
build up my leg muscles.

It's almost like PE at school, except that Mrs Fetlock isn't here to slave-drive me. She's a maniac when it comes to PE. She joins in with everything, which is fine most of the time, but sometimes we have piggyback races. I'll leave it to your imagination.

At least I'm back on my feet – I mean foot. I have to use crutches. Don't tell anyone but they're quite fun once you're used to them. They're good for poking things. The other advantage to being allowed up is that I can wear ordinary clothes. My mum laughed when I got my favourite baggy jeans a few months ago but they're brilliant if your leg's in plaster. Anyway, I'm out of pyjamas at last. I feel so much more . . . um, like a person, I suppose.

Maybe that's why I don't like being in hospital. You end up feeling like an object, like something that has to be wrapped and unwrapped and cleaned and tidied and sorted. Next time your mum or dad says to you: 'Time you were out of bed. Come on, get up!' just remember that you can actually do that. You *can* get up. Most people in hospital can't.

It's been a great morning. When the doc had

seen me he left me sitting on my bed and went across to Kirsty and examined her chart. He went to her side and took her pulse. He pulled back both her eyelids and shone his little torch into her pupils. He told her to stick out her tongue and say 'ah'. He walked round her bed and took the pulse from her other arm.

By this time Princess La-La looked positively queasy. She was sure it was Bad News. The doctor showed the chart to Tricia, pointed out something and Tricia nodded gravely.

They whispered together and Tricia raised her eyebrows.

'That is so terribly sad,' she exclaimed in a loud enough voice for everyone to hear.

Kirsty almost collapsed on the spot. Her round eyes were fixed on the doctor. She slid right down into the bed, pulling the covers up to her chin as if she were trying to hide from the ghastly truth.

'What is it? What's wrong?'

The doctor took her hand, patted it gently and gave her a pitying look. 'I'm afraid it's bad news.'

'What is it?'

'According to your chart here, you're dead.'

Princess La-La sat bolt upright and gave an anguished wail. 'I'm de–' she began, and then stopped, mid-word. She collapsed back against her pillow. You could almost hear the clickety-clack of her eyebrows as they knitted themselves into a furious frown.

'That's a horrible trick. How could you?' she demanded.

The doctor shrugged. 'I didn't, but someone has been tinkering with your chart. Look, the wiggly line here shows your temperature. You see where it changes colour? Someone has taken a pen and added a bit extra so according to this your temperature is over fifty degrees centigrade. That means your blood would have boiled and you would probably have exploded. Very messy.'

The doctor eyed Liam and me. 'Very funny, and when I tell my colleagues they'll laugh themselves silly. However, it was a stupid and dangerous thing to do. Never fiddle with these charts. They are for staff only. I don't want to know who did this. It doesn't matter. What does matter is that you understand how serious this might have been. It won't happen again – will it?'

Liam and I mumbled our agreement and he gave a nod. 'Good, that's the end of the matter. Just one thing, nurse. Do you think you could resuscitate Kirsty? A glass of fruit juice should be sufficient.'

Everyone laughed, except Princess La-La, who sat there looking like Miss Grumpy 2007. She folded her arms across her chest and her lower lip pouted so much you could almost stack books on it.

'Try and smile, Kirsty,' suggested the doctor. 'You should be relieved.'

As soon as the doc had gone Princess La-La pushed back her covers and came straight over. 'It was you, wasn't it?' she hissed. All I had to do was point at my broken leg. How could I possibly have done it? Anyhow, I didn't care. I was going home! I was on my way, almost.

Princess La-La went and accused Liam but he told her he didn't have any pens or pencils. 'Besides, I'm dyslexic,' he added, for good measure. Kirsty was so cross she didn't even realize dyslexia had nothing to do with it. He might just as easily have told her he had a pimple. She returned angrily to her bed, slumped into it, turned her back on us and that was that. Liam looked cheerily across at me and raised his thumb. I gave him an uneasy smile. Seeing Princess La-La miserable all the time was unsettling. It must be horrible to have so many food allergies and getting teased by Liam and me was hardly likely to cheer her up, even if she did seem to be asking for it.

On the other hand my heart was singing because I'm up and about today, hooray! Maisie was quite impressed when she came wandering in with her mum.

'It's a miracle! I'm cured!' I joked and we all laughed, even Maisie's mum.

'Yes, I heard all about that miracle of Maisie's yesterday. I know you two have something to do together but I wanted to pop in to thank you.'

'What for?'

'For getting Maisie talking.'

'I didn't do anything,' I said.

'You are the only person she has spoken to in almost a year. She says you told her something that got her talking. What on earth was it?'

Good grief! The body beneath the tins! Maisie had told her mum! Sweat broke out on my brow. I started to panic and glanced accusingly at Maisie, but she was shaking her head and mouthing 'NO!' at me. My heart decided to stop thundering along like a racehorse and return to normal.

'Don't think I can remember,' I said, and tried

to change the subject. 'Look, I've got crutches. Liam reckons I should stick go-faster stripes on them.'

'He's an idiot,' Maisie said, and her mother drew in her breath sharply.

'Maisie – don't say such things.'

I looked at her sympathetically. 'I'm afraid Maisie's right.' I called across the ward. 'Hey, Liam, you're an idiot, aren't you?'

'Course I am,' he answered. 'Grade A. Got a certificate and everything.'

Maisie's mum laughed and said she thought we were probably all idiots on this ward. 'Except for that girl over there. She's very quiet.'

'That's Kirsty,' I murmured.

'She does look poorly,' Maisie's mum said sympathetically. Maisie rolled her eyes.

'Of course she looks poorly, Mum. That's why she's in hospital. She hasn't come for a holiday.'

I couldn't help laughing and fortunately Maisie's mum joined in.

'I still can't get used to you talking, Maisie,' she said. 'It's so wonderful.'

'Gerroff,' said Maisie, trying to escape a hug, but I could see she was pleased really. 'Jack has got some school stuff to do and I said I'd help him, and you've got to go and see that psycho-whatsit person upstairs, so I'll see you back here in half an hour or so.'

'OK,' said her mum and I wondered who was in charge of who.

As soon as her mother had disappeared Maisie and I got down to business. First stop, Casualty. I explained my plan as we went.

'Let me ask the questions.'

'What do I do?' Maisie demanded.

'Follow my lead, and if you think of any good questions then ask them.'

Walking to Casualty was my first real outing since getting back on my feet and I felt quite proud of myself. Maisie went ahead opening doors for me. We had to go down loads of long corridors. Some were flat and some were sloping so that wheelchairs and beds could be pushed around without any problem. There was a long ramp up to Casualty which was a bit like conquering Everest, but I made it.

A wheelchair was parked right outside the door and as I tried to get past I got the end of one crutch caught on the side of the chair and then stuck in the spokes. Finally, when I had a third go, it plonked itself on the footbrake. Fiddly things, crutches. They take a bit of getting used to, I can tell you.

Casualty wasn't at all like my ward. It was busy, busy, busy, with loads of people waiting to be examined or have X-rays and so on. I even saw a kid with a teaspoon stuck up one nostril – made me feel quite normal. Maybe I wasn't so clumsy after all. There was no way I'd be so stupid as to get a teaspoon stuck up my nose.

We went across to Reception to see if it was all right to ask some questions for my project in between them dealing with patients, and the nurse said she'd do her best and asked what it was about.

'I'm doing a bar chart on admissions,' I explained. 'I need some figures. The hospital teacher, Miss Crispin, she told me to find out numbers for a particular day and we've chosen the day I was admitted, September 6th. How many people came in that day?'

The nurse searched the computer. 'Ninety-three, but they're not all admitted to hospital.

Most of them get treatment and then go home.'

'How many were admitted?' I asked.

'Twenty-five.'

'How many had broken bones?'

'Oh, goodness, what a lot of questions.
Thirteen suspected broken bones.'

'How many were dead?' Maisie demanded
eagerly, and there was a rustling noise as several
people in the waiting area put their newspapers
down. Faces swivelled in our direction.

'Dead?' repeated the nurse.

'Yes. I bet you had some dead bodies.'

'I don't think we need to discuss that.'

Maisie wasn't happy. 'We do. Jack and I need to know.' The waiting room was all ears now and Maisie was determined to find out more. 'I think we should be told. You must get dead bodies sometimes. What do you do with them? Do you have a bonfire?'

The nurse was horrified. 'Really! I'm sorry, I don't think I can . . .'

'You must!' interrupted Maisie. 'I bet someone was brought in on September 6th and they died. Maybe they'd been in an accident, like a *tomato*-related accident,' she hinted.

'I think you'd better stop,' said the nurse coldly, but now some of the patients had joined us.

'What's this about bonfires for the dead?' asked an old lady. 'That's dreadful, that is. I wouldn't have come here if I'd known you had bonfires.'

'We don't!' insisted the nurse. 'It's this girl here, she –'

'Fancy blaming a sweet little child like this,' blustered the old lady. 'Goodness gracious, what is the world coming to? Well, I can tell you something,' she added, almost stabbing the nurse with an accusatory finger, 'I'm not stopping here just so's I end up on your bonfire! I'm going to take my blister somewhere else, so put that in your pipe and smoke it!'

The old woman barged off towards the door, calling out to the remaining patients as she went, 'I'd get out of here if I were you, before you all end up on one of their flaming conflagrations!'

'We're going!' muttered several patients. 'I don't want a conflagration, do you? Last time I was here I had an injection – that was bad enough. I'm not staying for no conflagration.'

'It's . . . I . . . you . . . we . . .!' stuttered the reception nurse. 'Come back! There aren't any bonfires! There isn't a problem!' But nobody was listening to her and the exodus continued. The nurse glared at Maisie. 'Do you see what you've done?' she cried.

'It's not my fault,' said Maisie. 'We just need an answer to our questions. How many people got crushed on September 6th?' I started to pull her away from the desk and she yelled back at the nurse, 'Go on, tell us! I bet someone got crushed. Maybe a tomato fell . . .'

I clamped a hand over her mouth. 'Shut up!
Leave it!' I tried to hurry her out of Casualty.
As we reached the door it was flung open and a
doctor staggered in, clutching his head. There
was a large gash on his forehead. He pushed
past us and I heard the nurse exclaim, 'Doctor
Guptal! What on earth happened to your head?'

'I was mown down by a runaway wheelchair,'
he snapped back. 'It came hurtling down the
ramp out there and knocked me flying. Someone
must have left the brake off.'

I hurried after Maisie.

11 How Princess La-La Saved My Life

I'm going mad waiting to be arrested. If this goes on much longer I think I'll go to the nearest police station and give myself up. It's either that or leave the country.

It's two days since Maisie and I went to Casualty and she hasn't been back since. Tyler had an operation yesterday and he's either had the curtains round his bed or he's been fast asleep. Tyler's the latest guest at Hotel Hospital. Liam's gone and Tyler's arrived. Liam went yesterday morning. His parents came and helped him pack. I'm going to miss him.

Time was really dragging. I was desperate for something to do and in the end I went and played 'Scissors, Paper, Stone' with Princess La-La. Unfortunately she's much better than me. We started off doing best of five, but she was still winning so I said best of eleven and so on. I gave up when we got to best of forty-nine. I was too far behind.

'What does that stuff taste of?' I asked, pointing at the bowl beside her bed.

'Not a lot,' she shrugged.

'It looks horrible.'

'It's not as horrible as throwing up every time I eat something I'm allergic to,' she said.

'I guess not.' It was hard to imagine food making you ill and miserable. I like eating. Don't know what I'd do if I was like Kirsty, with all those allergies.

'You'll be going home soon, then?'

'Few more days,' I nodded. 'Got to do more physio first. How about you?'

'I have to do some tests with the dietician and then I can go home for the time being.'

'Will you have to come back?'

Kirsty nodded. 'This is my seventh stay.' Seventh! No wonder she always looked fed up.

'Wouldn't it be easier to live here all the time?' I asked.

'Is that what you'd like to do?' she flashed back.

'It was only a joke.'

Kirsty gave a sour glance. 'I don't think

hospitals are very jokey places.'

'Of course not. That's the point. You've got to have jokes otherwise you'd go mad.'

'Making jokes hasn't stopped you going mad. You're the maddest person in the building, now that crazy Maisie has gone.' There was a little smile on her face.

'See?' I said triumphantly. 'You've just made a joke and it's cheered you up. You're almost smiling.'

The smile vanished instantly. I thought it was

because of what I'd just said but Kirsty was staring over my shoulder towards the desk. I swung round to look and my heart stopped dead on the spot. If I'd been fixed up to one of those cardiogram thingies it would have been flatlining and everyone would be rushing round giving mouth-to-mouth and all that stuff.

Two policemen were at the desk. One was talking to Tricia and the other was gazing carefully round the ward. His eyes fixed on me and there they stopped. Tricia brought them over.

'Jack, these policemen would like a word with you. Give me a shout if you need me. I think your parents were meant to be here but they seem to be late. Maybe Kirsty will keep an eye on them for you,' and she winked at both of us. Ha ha. Very funny.

I could hardly bring myself to look the policemen in the face. It was as if their eyes were speaking to me, saying: *We have you now, Jack Lemming. We have tracked you down and you're heading for the slammer.* There was no way any miracle was going to rescue me this time.

'You two are an item then, are you?'

'NO WAY!' we chorused, looked at each other in surprise and turned deep red. One of the policemen got out a notepad and licked his pencil.

'My mum says you shouldn't lick pencils because you get brain damage,' Kirsty said.

'Is that right?' said the policeman.

'I don't know. I'm just telling you what my mum says. She also says carrots make you see in the dark but I don't believe her. If it were true rabbits wouldn't get run over.'

'That's very interesting, Kirsty, but we need to

ask your friend some questions.'

'He's not my friend. He's only eleven.'

The taller officer glanced wearily at his companion, who shrugged and said: 'That's the trouble with patients. They're getting younger all the time.' They both chuckled and the tall officer turned back to me.

'Now then, Jack, cast your mind back to your accident. Was the car you crashed into moving?'

'No. I don't think there was anyone in it. I told the other man all that.'

'What other man?'

'Mr Cutter.'

'Oh yes. He's not with us, though. Mr Cutter works for the insurance company involved. The accident details were reported to the police so we have to ask our own questions. Why didn't you see the car you crashed into?'

'I was riding fast.'

'I guessed that. You wouldn't have broken your leg if you'd been riding slowly. But why didn't you see the car even if you were riding fast?'

Think, brain, think! Quick, think of something! 'I was looking back over my shoulder.'

'Ah. Now that makes sense. What were you

looking for?'

Think again! Come on, get yourself into gear, brain!
What could I tell them? How could I say I
thought everyone was after me because I'd
just killed an old man by burying him under
a tomato landslide? 'I thought I'd dropped
something.'

'From your shopping?'

'I thought I'd dropped the milk.'

'And had you?'

'I don't know.' That was weird actually. What *had* happened to the milk? It must have got lost in the crash because I never saw it again. Maybe somebody found it after the mess had been cleared – they saw it and they thought, 'Hmmm, free milk! I'll have that.' And they took it. They stole my milk!

'The milk was stolen,' I said flatly.

'You'd stolen the milk? That was why you were riding so fast? You were making a getaway?' pressed the policeman.

'No!' I was panicking.

Princess La-La gave a deep sigh. 'Jack means he dropped the milk when he crashed and it was never found. Maybe somebody saw it and took it.' We all looked at her – me gratefully, and the policemen with surprise.

'Ah, yes, of course. Let's forget the milk then and go back to the accident. Do you know how much damage you caused?'

I could feel the blood drain from my face. I've no idea where it went after that. I swallowed hard and shook my head. So did the policeman asking all the questions.

116

'It was very bad, Jack. Very, very bad.'

'I don't think it was much fun for Jack either,' put in the princess sharply. 'He's been in hospital for five weeks with a broken leg. It's not a holiday camp here, you know. Have you got any more questions? Jack's tired and he needs his rest.'

The two policemen looked at each other. One put his notebook away. 'That'll be all for now,' he said. They nodded at each of us and went clomping off. Kirsty watched them depart.

'You look as if you've seen a ghost,' she said. 'Maybe several.'

'Thanks for getting rid of them,' I managed to mutter rather hoarsely.

'Policemen are supposed to be helpful,' she said. 'But they scared me.'

'Me too. I'd better get back to bed. Thanks.'

My mind was in a whirl. So many questions. Why hadn't the police arrested me? Were they trying to trick me into a confession? Why hadn't they said anything about the body in the supermarket? Were they trying to find out how much I knew? And then there was Kirsty – what was all that about? Why had she stuck up for me like that? I was beginning to feel a bit rotten about the tricks Liam and I had played.

Things were such a muddle. I had been hoping that as time went by things would become clearer, but instead they were just getting more and more confused.

12 How to Win a Holiday

I've been practising my walking. I'm getting better all the time and I'm pretty nifty with the old crutches. I use them to push open doors, flick light switches from a long distance – all sorts. I even used one of them to play pool with Tyler. He's not as much fun as Liam was.

There's a pool table in the lounge area but there's only one cue, so Tyler used that and I used one of my crutches – and I won. Result! Tyler said it didn't count because I wasn't using a proper cue.

'I know, but that makes it more difficult.'

'No, because it's fatter at the end. My cue's tiny.'

'OK, give me the cue and you use my crutch.'

'I'm not using your stinking crutch! I might catch something.'

'You can't catch a broken leg,' I pointed out. 'You're just a bad loser.'

'No, you cheated, and you're a pain.' Tyler went back to his bed. He's a bit thorny, Tyler. He seems to like arguing.

One thing about hospitals is that when anyone has an argument you never see them storming off. That's because most of the time they can't. You can't storm off if you've got a broken leg, or stitches in your side, or you're attached to a drip. Arguments last longer in hospital. And if you're trapped on a ward with someone you don't like – that's murder! In fact I'm amazed there aren't thousands of murders taking place in hospitals. You'd think the corridors would be full of bodies battered to death with crutches, stabbed with scalpels, throttled with bandages – not to mention being mown down by hit-and-run wheelchairs. (Oops!) Glad I'm going home!

And I AM going home. The doc says I can go tomorrow. Escape! Freedom! At last! Acne-Man seems pretty pleased too.

'Hooray. I'm fed up with all your moaning.' He plumped up my pillow.

'I don't moan,' I moaned. 'How's your girlfriend?'

'What girlfriend?'

'Kathy.'

Acne-Man blushed. Brilliant – red ears, the lot! He carried on plumping my pillow, banging it with one fist. I'd never seen a pillow plumped up so much.

'You do like her, don't you?'

'None of your business.'

'Well, she likes you,' I told him. 'Maisie told me.'

'Crazy Maisie? Huh! What does she know about it?'

'Kathy told her, of course.'

Acne-Man stopped. He couldn't help smiling. He tried to hide it but I could tell he was pleased.

'Like I said, it's none of your business.'

'Will you marry her?'

'Jack – shut up.'

I started to hum 'Here Comes the Bride' but Acne-Man threatened to put the pillow over my head and smother me. Then, talk of the devil, both Maisie and Kathy appeared. Maisie was bouncing around like her legs were pogo sticks while Kathy and Acne-Man made moony faces at each other and drifted across to the desk.

'Look at them,' I said. 'Makes you want to throw up.'

'It's lovely.' Maisie sighed.

'Yuk. What are you doing back here, anyway?'

'I came back to see you. Mum's waiting for me in the lounge. I've got something to show you – something important.' Maisie's eyes were shining and she was beaming from ear to ear. 'Guess what happened yesterday?'

'I don't know. You went back to Mars?'

'Stupid!'

'Tell me then.'

'We had fish and chips.'

'Wow! Fish and chips! And you've come all the way back to the hospital just to tell me. I am so pleased, Maisie. Fancy that, fish and chips.'

Maisie ignored my sarcasm and calmly waited until I'd finished. Then she shoved her hand into her little bag and pulled out a bit of newspaper.

'The fish and chips were wrapped in this,' she explained.

'Yeah, I can smell it from here. Urgh, it's all greasy, Maisie. Take it away. It's foul. What did you bring that in for?'

'If you let me finish I'll tell you. Look. See for yourself.'

She spread the paper on my bed and jabbed a finger at a headline.

LUCKY TOMATOES WIN HOLIDAY FOR ALF

Alfred Butler had no idea what was in store for him when he visited his local supermarket last week. He was standing beside a giant mountain of tinned tomatoes when the pile collapsed, pinning Alfred beneath them. The display was part of a holiday promotion where shoppers had to guess how many tins were in the pile in order to win a holiday by the Italian Lakes. Startled shoppers rushed to the rescue and Alfred was pulled unharmed from beneath the wreckage. The store awarded him the holiday. Supermarket Manager Keith Townsend said: 'We felt we had to give Alf the prize after the dreadful accident. He may not have known the exact number of tins in the mountain, but he certainly felt their full weight!'

'Jack? Jack? Are you all right? Jack?'

Maisie's voice sounded as if it was coming from somewhere far, far away. I felt as if a huge tide had just surged through my entire body from top to toe and back again, and now it was sloshing about inside me, slowly flattening out. I opened my eyes.

'What's the matter?' whispered Maisie. 'Why are you crying?'

'I'm not,' I said, brushing my eyes with the back of my hand, and I read the paper again. And again.

'Everything's all right,' grinned Maisie.

'So why have the police and that Cutter man been questioning me?'

Maisie shrugged, a trifle crossly. 'Don't ask me. Honestly, I thought you'd be pleased. You look as miserable as the man I saw in Casualty on the way here.'

'What was wrong with him?'

'He had a dinner fork stuck in his bum.'

You see? It's not just me! These things really do happen to people. Maybe I'm not so clumsy after all. And I hadn't managed to kill anyone either. That was some relief, I can tell you. I felt like I was pumped full of helium, light enough to float away into the blue. Brilliant!

I was a bit cross about that man winning the holiday, though. He might have shared the prize with me. After all, if it hadn't been for me the tins wouldn't have fallen over in the first place. He should have taken me with him.

I was pleased to see Maisie again, not just because of the newspaper, but seeing her was good. It made me feel that bad things could happen but they didn't have to stay bad. Sometimes they could get better, with a bit of help.

It was strange leaving hospital behind after I'd been in so long. Obviously it was great to be going, but there was a bit of sadness too, because I knew so many people there. Kathy and Tricia insisted on kissing me goodbye, which was incredibly embarrassing.

'Ah!' said Mum. 'Look how red Jack is!' Ben started sniggering. He's so pathetic.

'Yeah, well, Kathy should be kissing him, not me,' I said, pointing at Acne-Man. 'They're always snogging.' That stopped them all in their tracks. Ha ha! Got them! Ben whooped with laughter and Dad coughed very loudly and said

he'd bring the car to the front of the building.

We were about to go when I saw Princess La-La looking my way, scowling as usual. I left the others and went across.

'You're going then?'

'Yep.'

'Everybody's going,' she murmured. 'Liam, you –'

'Your turn next, I hope.'

'Maybe. Next week apparently. Anyhow, I don't want to see you in here ever again.'

'I don't want to see YOU in here ever again,'

I said. 'I hope you get better; hope you're out of here soon.'

'Thanks.'

'Take it easy, princess.'

'Princess?' she squawked. I bit my tongue. She'd never known about her nickname. I couldn't tell her now.

'Why not? What's wrong with princess?' I said.

'You're not chatting me up, are you?'

'Get out of here!'

Kirsty almost smiled. She pointed at the door. 'No, you get out of here.'

So I did.

Ashley and Kathy came to the hospital exit to say goodbye. When we got to the car Ben opened the door for me. Unfortunately he forgot I was on crutches and couldn't move as quickly as usual. The door knocked one of my crutches flying and I staggered back on one leg, hopping furiously, trying to stay upright. I knew I was going to fall. I already knew what was going to happen. I was going to go right over, crash to the ground, break my leg again and get whisked straight back inside.

'Got you!' Two strong arms caught me and

held me tight. It was Dad. He glanced at Ben
who, I'm pleased to say, had turned white.

'Nice try, Ben,' joked Dad. 'But I'm afraid Jack
is definitely coming home.'

There was a faint cheer and burst of clapping.
I looked back at the hospital. Kathy and Acne-
Man were clapping and smiling. My eye was
caught by a movement above their heads. On the
floor above them, waving from behind a window,
was Kirsty. I waved back and climbed into the
car.

Ben groaned. 'Do you have to put your leg right across the whole car?' he complained.

'It's broken,' I said.

'What have you come out of hospital for then? If it's broken you should still be inside. You're taking up all the room. Mum, tell Jack to move his leg. Dad, Jack's a pain. Can't we take him back? He says his leg's still broken. Take him back. Dad? Mum?'

I stared out of the car window and smiled. It was so good to be going home.

Ask Jeremy

Of all the books you have written, which one is your favourite?

I loved writing both **KRAZY KOW SAVES THE WORLD – WELL, ALMOST** and **STUFF**, my first book for teenagers. Both these made me laugh out loud while I was writing and I was pleased with the overall result in each case. I also love writing the stories about Nicholas and his daft family – **MY DAD**, **MY MUM**, **MY BROTHER** and so on.

If you couldn't be a writer what would you be?

Well, I'd be pretty fed up for a start, because writing was the one thing I knew I wanted to do from the age of nine onward. But if I DID have to do something else, I would love to be either an accomplished pianist or an artist of some sort. Music and art have played a big part in my whole life and I would love to be involved in them in some way.

What's the best thing about writing stories?

Oh dear – so many things to say here! Getting paid for making things up is pretty high on the list! It's also something you do on your own, inside your own head – nobody can interfere with that. The only boss you have is yourself. And you are creating something that nobody else has made before you. I also love making my readers laugh and want to read more and more.

Did you ever have a nightmare teacher?
(And who was your best ever?)

My nightmare at primary school was Mrs Chappell, long since dead. I knew her secret – she was not actually human. She was a Tyrannosaurus rex in disguise. She taught me for two years when I was in Y5 and Y6, and we didn't like each other at all. My best ever was when I was in Y3 and Y4. Her name was Miss Cox, and she was the one who first encouraged me to write stories. She was brilliant. Sadly, she is long dead too.

When you were a kid you used to play kiss-chase. Did you always do the chasing or did anyone ever chase you?!

I usually did the chasing, but when I got chased, I didn't bother to run very fast! Maybe I shouldn't admit to that! We didn't play kiss-chase at school – it was usually played during holidays. If we had tried playing it at school we would have been in serious trouble. Mind you, I seemed to spend most of my time in trouble of one sort or another, so maybe it wouldn't have mattered that much.

14½ Things You Didn't Know About

Jeremy Strong

* * * * * * * * * * * * * * * * * * *

1. He loves eating liquorice.

2. He used to like diving. He once dived from the high board and his trunks came off!

3. He used to play electric violin in a rock band called **THE INEDIBLE CHEESE SANDWICH.**

4. He got a 100-metre swimming certificate when he couldn't even swim.

5. When he was five, he sat on a heater and burnt his bottom.

6. Jeremy used to look after a dog that kept eating his underpants. (No – **NOT** while he was wearing them!)

7. When he was five, he left a basin tap running with the plug in and flooded the bathroom.

8. He can make his ears waggle.

9. He has visited over a thousand schools.

10. He once scored minus ten in an exam! That's ten less than nothing!

11. His hair has gone grey, but his mind hasn't.

12. He'd like to have a pet tiger.

13. He'd like to learn the piano.

14. He has dreadful handwriting.

And a half . . . His favourite hobby is sleeping. He's very good at it.

This is the first story about my crazy family. We're not all crazy of course – it's Dad mostly. I mean, who would think of bringing home an alligator as a pet? It got into our next-door neighbour's garden and ate all the fish from his pond. It even got into his car! That gave him quite a surprise, I can tell you! He was not very happy about it. Mum says Crunchbag will have to go, but Dad and I quite like him, even if his teeth are rather big and sharp.

* * * * * * * * * * * * * * * * * * *

Big problems in my family – we're running out of money fast. Dad reckons we should start up our own mini-farm. But the yoghurt we made exploded, and the goat needed an aromatherapy massage!

That's the sort of daft thing that happens in my family. And then my baby bro, Cheese (yes – I know Cheese is a very odd name for a baby!), was spotted on national television showing off his bottom!

Woofy hi! I'm Streaker, the fastest dog in the world.
My owner, Trevor, thinks he can train me to obey him.
The trouble is even I don't know what I'm going to do
next! I don't know what SIT or STOP mean, and I do
get into some big scrapes. We almost got
arrested once! This is the first book about
me and it's almost as funny and fast
as I am!

LAUGH YOUR Socks off with

THE HUNDRED-
MILE-AN-HOUR DOG

Available Now!

* * * * * * * * * * * * * * * * * * *

I'm Jamie. I am going to be the world's greatest film
director when I grow up. I'm trying to make a film
about a cartoon cow I've invented called KRAZY KOW.
However, making a film isn't as easy as you might
think. How was I to know everyone would see the bit
where I caught my big sister snogging Justin? How
was I to know the exploding strawberries would make
quite so much mess? How was I to know my big bro's
football kit would turn pink? And why did everyone
have to blame ME?

LAUGH YOUR Socks off with

KRAZY KOW
SAVES THE
WORLD –
WELL, ALMOST

Available Now!